BRASS BUTTON

BY

CRESCENT DRAGONWAGON

ILLUSTRATED BY

SUSAN PARADISE

ATHENEUM BOOKS FOR YOUNG READERS

Atheneum Books for Young Readers
An imprint of Simon & Schuster Children's Publishing Division
1230 Avenue of the Americas
New York, New York 10020
Book design by Becky Terhune
The text of this book is set in Bembo.
The illustrations are rendered in gouache.
Printed in the United States of America
First Edition
10 9 8 7 6 5 4 3 2 1
Library of Congress Cataloging-in-Publication Data
Dragonwagon, Crescent.
Brass button / by Crescent Dragonwagon ; illustrated by Susan Paradise.—1st ed.
p. cm.
Summary: When a brass button falls off Mrs. Moffatt's new coat,
it begins a journey around the neighborhood and eventually
ends up back where it began.
ISBN 0-689-80582-9
[1. Buttons—Fiction. 2. Friendship—Fiction.]
I. Paradise, Susan, ill. II. Title.
PZ7.D7824Br 1997
[Fic]—dc20
95-43893

For Aunt Dot and Jim Cherry,
a *most* original couple.
—C. D.

For my children, "Shank," Lisa, and Sean, with
love and appreciation. For Virginia Evans and
Carolyn Coman, with special gratitude for
their consistent love and support.
—S. P.

CHAPTER ONE

On the first day of spring, Mrs. Moffatt bought a
new red coat with six shiny brass buttons. The coat
was on sale because winter was almost over, and not
many people were buying coats. However, there were
still a few cold days, and on them Mrs. Moffatt wore
her new coat. It was so red it made her happy, and she
loved the big brass buttons, large as silver dollars.

One April day, when it was really too warm for a red wool coat, Mrs. Moffatt wore her new coat anyway, and was hot all day long. Walking home from work, Mrs. Moffatt had to take off her coat, and she came up Oak Street with it over one arm. She stopped to talk to Mr. George Peterson, her neighbor, a retired architect, who was out pulling away dead leaves from his tulips.

Their conversation touched on Swiss chocolate, La Jolla, California, and Mr. Peterson's uncle Phineas, who did silk embroidery. Their discussion was so interesting that Mrs. Moffatt did not notice that the thorny branches of one of Mr. Peterson's raspberry bushes caught the thread of the bottom button and pulled it off her beautiful red coat.

When Mrs. Moffatt came inside, she still didn't notice the missing button. Instead, she said to herself sternly, "Now, Jane, as much as you love your new coat, you must put it away until it gets cold enough to wear it again." So she did, hanging the coat, with its five shiny brass buttons, big as silver dollars, in her downstairs closet, to wait until the next cold day.

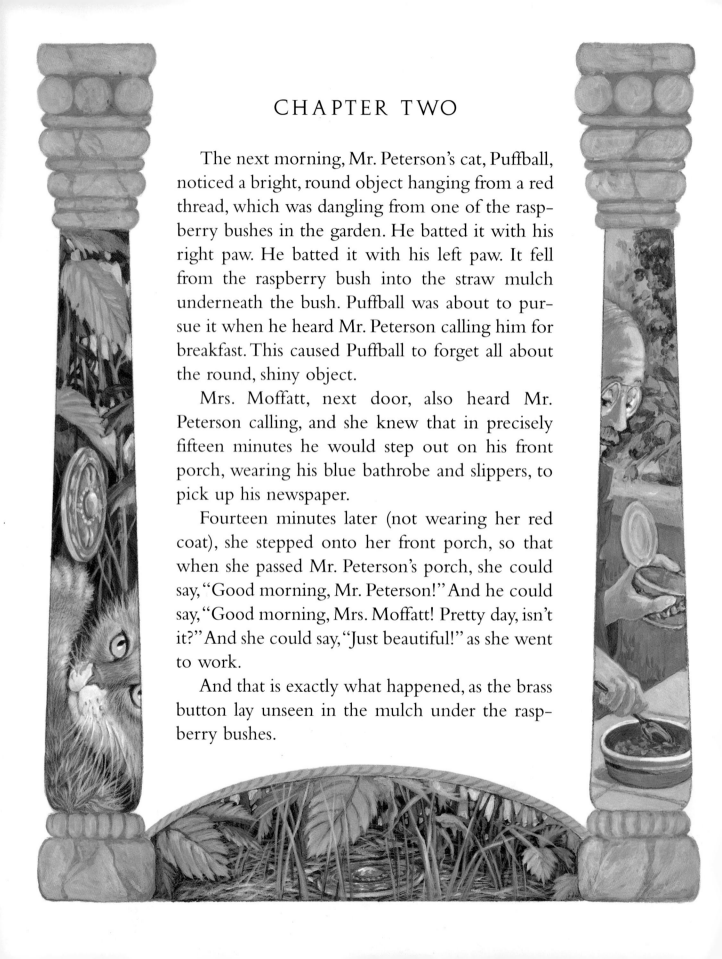

CHAPTER TWO

The next morning, Mr. Peterson's cat, Puffball, noticed a bright, round object hanging from a red thread, which was dangling from one of the raspberry bushes in the garden. He batted it with his right paw. He batted it with his left paw. It fell from the raspberry bush into the straw mulch underneath the bush. Puffball was about to pursue it when he heard Mr. Peterson calling him for breakfast. This caused Puffball to forget all about the round, shiny object.

Mrs. Moffatt, next door, also heard Mr. Peterson calling, and she knew that in precisely fifteen minutes he would step out on his front porch, wearing his blue bathrobe and slippers, to pick up his newspaper.

Fourteen minutes later (not wearing her red coat), she stepped onto her front porch, so that when she passed Mr. Peterson's porch, she could say, "Good morning, Mr. Peterson!" And he could say, "Good morning, Mrs. Moffatt! Pretty day, isn't it?" And she could say, "Just beautiful!" as she went to work.

And that is exactly what happened, as the brass button lay unseen in the mulch under the raspberry bushes.

CHAPTER THREE

One Monday in May, it rained all day long, a hard, cold, gray rain. Mrs. Moffatt wore her yellow slicker. It was raining too hard for her to say hello to Mr. Peterson, who ran out and in as quickly as he could to get his paper.

But that night when she came home, Mr. Peterson had left a message on her answering machine, inviting her to his house for a dinner of vegetable soup and homemade biscuits. As they ate dinner, they talked about English cream cake, Little Rock, Arkansas, and Mrs. Moffatt's aunt Lucretia, who believed one should always say "Rabbit, rabbit" first thing in the morning on the first day of each month, and especially on the first day of the new year, for good luck.

Then, as Puffball dozed on an ottoman, they played Parcheesi. Little did they know that outside, the rain had washed away some of the mulch and formed a small gully, and that in this gully the brass button from Mrs. Moffatt's red wool coat was floating away down Oak Street.

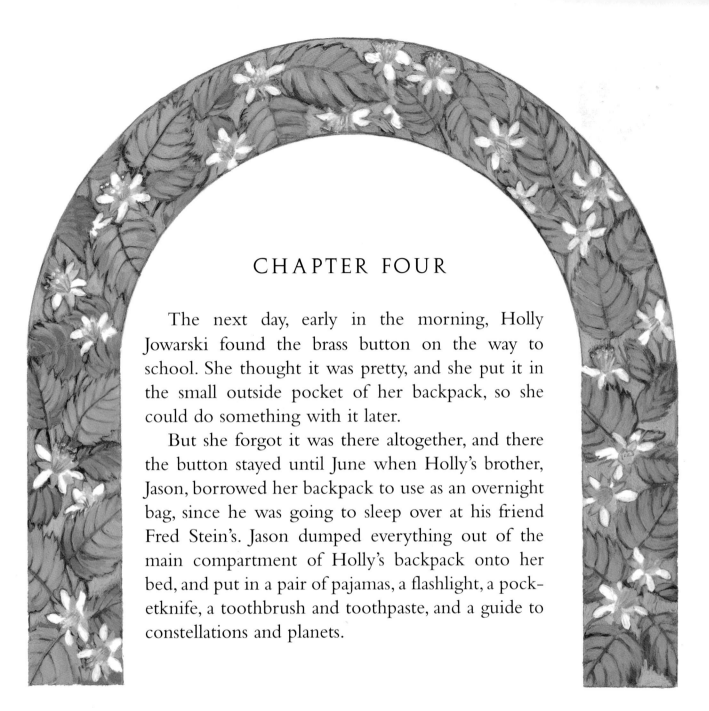

CHAPTER FOUR

The next day, early in the morning, Holly Jowarski found the brass button on the way to school. She thought it was pretty, and she put it in the small outside pocket of her backpack, so she could do something with it later.

But she forgot it was there altogether, and there the button stayed until June when Holly's brother, Jason, borrowed her backpack to use as an overnight bag, since he was going to sleep over at his friend Fred Stein's. Jason dumped everything out of the main compartment of Holly's backpack onto her bed, and put in a pair of pajamas, a flashlight, a pocketknife, a toothbrush and toothpaste, and a guide to constellations and planets.

But he forgot to open the small outside pocket of his sister Holly's backpack, where the forgotten brass button lay. So the brass button from Mrs. Moffatt's red coat traveled, hidden and secret, all the way to Fred Stein's.

Meanwhile, all this time Mr. Peterson was bringing Mrs. Moffatt things from his garden: lilacs in May, purple irises in June, and fresh blueberries in July. Mrs. Moffatt invited Mr. Peterson over for blueberry cobbler and vanilla ice cream, and he invited her to a Fourth of July picnic.

But Mrs. Moffatt already had plans. "I am going to the beach, George," she said.

"Oh? With friends?" asked Mr. Peterson.

"No, by myself," said Mrs. Moffatt.

"I admire that," said Mr. Peterson. "I myself have not traveled much since my wife, Amelia, died."

"Oh, but you should!" cried Mrs. Moffatt. "For an architect it is so important especially, to see all the building styles of the world! The pyramids of Egypt! The yurts of Tibet! Igloos, temples, mosques, huts, and palaces! Courtyards and conservatories!"

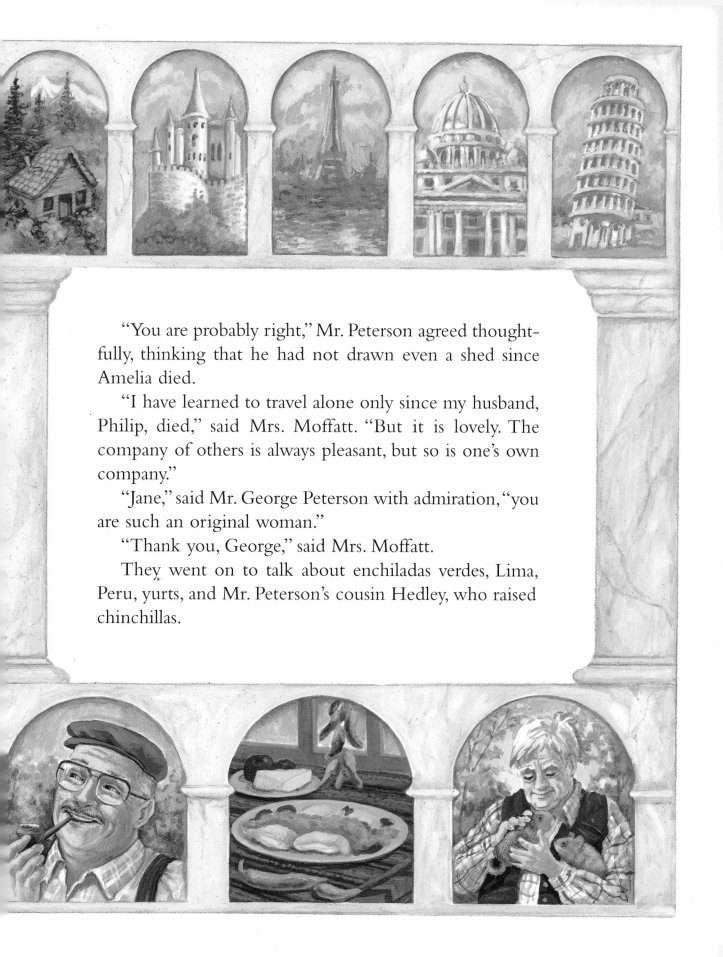

"You are probably right," Mr. Peterson agreed thoughtfully, thinking that he had not drawn even a shed since Amelia died.

"I have learned to travel alone only since my husband, Philip, died," said Mrs. Moffatt. "But it is lovely. The company of others is always pleasant, but so is one's own company."

"Jane," said Mr. George Peterson with admiration, "you are such an original woman."

"Thank you, George," said Mrs. Moffatt.

They went on to talk about enchiladas verdes, Lima, Peru, yurts, and Mr. Peterson's cousin Hedley, who raised chinchillas.

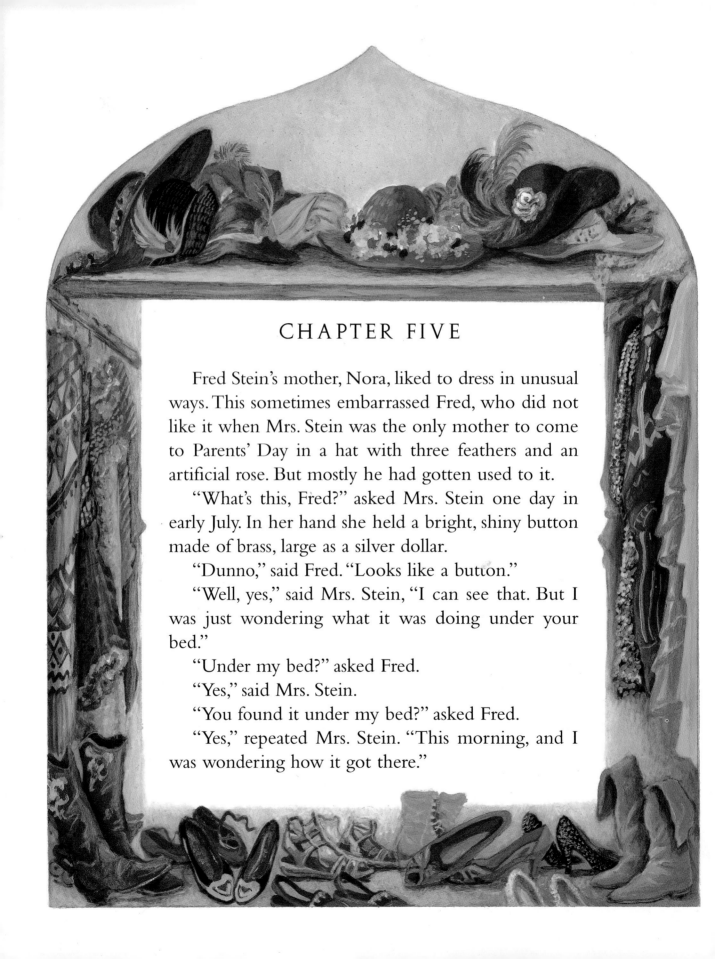

CHAPTER FIVE

Fred Stein's mother, Nora, liked to dress in unusual ways. This sometimes embarrassed Fred, who did not like it when Mrs. Stein was the only mother to come to Parents' Day in a hat with three feathers and an artificial rose. But mostly he had gotten used to it.

"What's this, Fred?" asked Mrs. Stein one day in early July. In her hand she held a bright, shiny button made of brass, large as a silver dollar.

"Dunno," said Fred. "Looks like a button."

"Well, yes," said Mrs. Stein, "I can see that. But I was just wondering what it was doing under your bed."

"Under my bed?" asked Fred.

"Yes," said Mrs. Stein.

"You found it under my bed?" asked Fred.

"Yes," repeated Mrs. Stein. "This morning, and I was wondering how it got there."

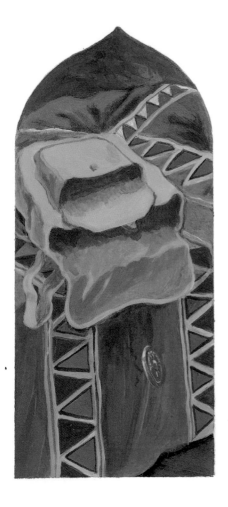

"Dunno," said Fred.

And he didn't. He didn't know that the brass button had traveled to his house in the outside pocket of Holly Jowarski's backpack, which his friend Jason Jowarski had brought over when he spent the night a month earlier. He didn't know that Jason had left the backpack on the edge of the bed, and that when the two boys went downstairs for dinner, the brass button fell out of the small outside pocket, dropped to the floor, and rolled under the bed to the farthest, hardest-to-find corner.

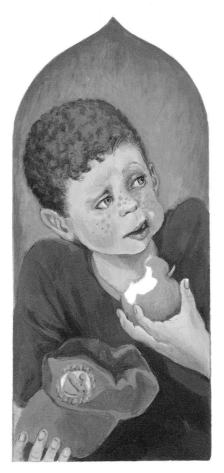

"Do you mind if I keep it?" Mrs. Stein asked Fred.

"Sure, you can have it," said Fred. Then he asked cautiously, "What are you going to do with it, Mom?"

"I thought I would sew it on my plain blue bathing suit," said Mrs. Stein dreamily. "In the middle, at the neckline. That suit needs some livening up."

"Okay with me," said Fred, hoping his mother wouldn't liven up the suit too much.

CHAPTER SIX

The next day Mrs. Stein sewed the brass button onto her blue bathing suit. She thought it looked very nice. She added some red and white ruffles to the shoulders of the suit, too, since she was wearing it to the beach for the Fourth of July weekend. She was pleased with the results.

Mr. and Mrs. Stein, Fred, and Fred's friend Jason Jowarski all went to the beach together. They were eating their picnic lunch under a striped umbrella when Jason pointed to a lady reading under a red umbrella. "Hey, there's Mrs. Moffatt!" he said. "Hi, Mrs. Moffatt! Hi, Mrs. Moffatt!" He and Fred waved hard at the lady, who smiled, putting down her book to wave back.

"Who's that?" asked Mr. Stein.

"That's our art teacher," Fred told his father. "She's really nice."

"She lives down the street from me, too," added Jason.

Later Mrs. Moffatt came over to say hello. The Steins invited her to join them and share their picnic, but Mrs. Moffatt said no thank you.

She did not take particular notice of the shiny brass button, large as a silver dollar, on Mrs. Stein's blue bathing suit. She certainly did not think of it in connection with the pretty red coat she had bought herself way back on the first day of spring.

CHAPTER SEVEN

Mrs. Stein decided, after the Fourth of July weekend, that the brass button on the blue bathing suit was not entirely successful. Although it was very pretty, it pressed into her uncomfortably when she lay facedown on the sand. So, one day in August, she decided to take it off the bathing suit.

She carried her sewing basket, her scissors, and the suit out to the front porch. She had just snipped off the brass button when the phone rang inside the house. She stood up to get it, and the button fell off her lap and rolled across the porch.

"Darn," she said. When she came out again, after a long conversation with her sister in Topeka, she looked all over the porch for the button but could not find it. She even looked under the hydrangea bushes at the end of the porch, but she could not find the button anywhere. "Darn," she said again.

The reason she could not find the button was that it had rolled off the porch, through the hydrangeas, and onto the lawn, where it lay in the sun. It looked so bright and shiny that it attracted the attention of a large crow who picked it up in her beak and flew off with it to her nest, eight blocks away, in a large sycamore tree high above Mr. George Peterson's front yard on Oak Street.

CHAPTER EIGHT

It was pouring rain one cold, gray fall day, and Mrs. Jane Moffatt could only wave to Mr. George Peterson on her way to school. But that afternoon, when she came home from teaching, she found a message from Mr. Peterson on her answering machine, as she had suspected she would.

"I have made mulligatawny soup," said Mr. Peterson on the machine, "and pita bread toast. You have certainly broadened my horizons, Jane, and I hope you will do me the honor of sharing dinner with me tonight."

At the very moment Mrs. Jane Moffatt stood listening to the message on her answering machine, there was a sudden gust of wind and a sudden burst of rain. The crow's nest, long deserted by the crow, blew out of the sycamore tree and fell on the stone garden path leading to Mr. Peterson's front door. Out rolled the brass button, right onto the path. But Mrs. Moffatt, hurrying down the path later that day, to get into Mr. Peterson's warm kitchen and out of the rain, did not look down, and so she did not notice the button.

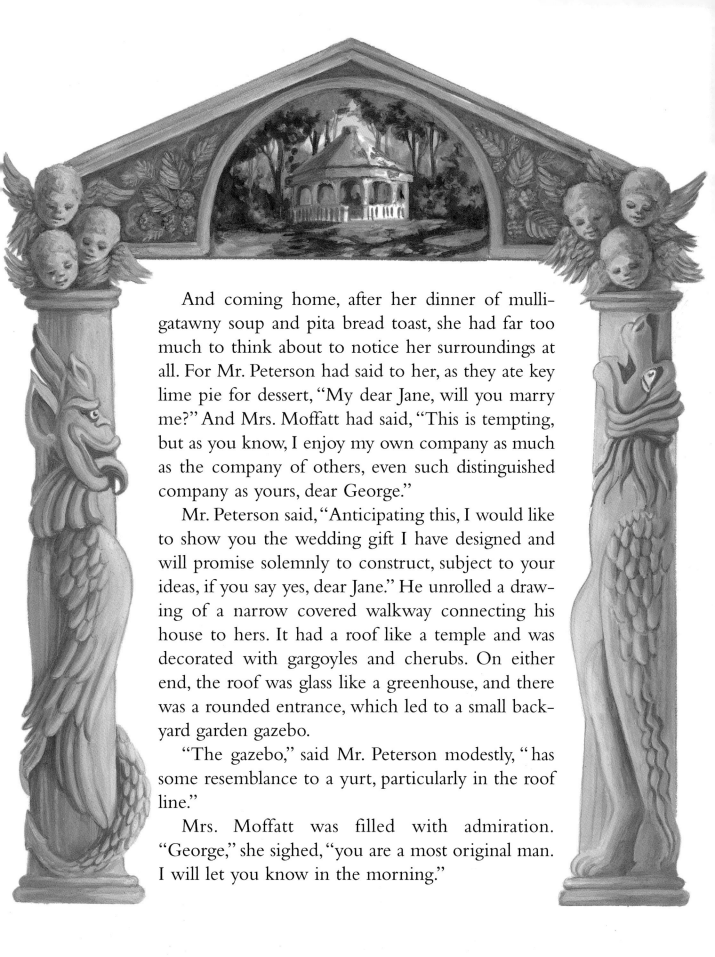

And coming home, after her dinner of mulligatawny soup and pita bread toast, she had far too much to think about to notice her surroundings at all. For Mr. Peterson had said to her, as they ate key lime pie for dessert, "My dear Jane, will you marry me?" And Mrs. Moffatt had said, "This is tempting, but as you know, I enjoy my own company as much as the company of others, even such distinguished company as yours, dear George."

Mr. Peterson said, "Anticipating this, I would like to show you the wedding gift I have designed and will promise solemnly to construct, subject to your ideas, if you say yes, dear Jane." He unrolled a drawing of a narrow covered walkway connecting his house to hers. It had a roof like a temple and was decorated with gargoyles and cherubs. On either end, the roof was glass like a greenhouse, and there was a rounded entrance, which led to a small backyard garden gazebo.

"The gazebo," said Mr. Peterson modestly, "has some resemblance to a yurt, particularly in the roof line."

Mrs. Moffatt was filled with admiration. "George," she sighed, "you are a most original man. I will let you know in the morning."

CHAPTER NINE

The next day dawned bright and clear, but very, very cold. Mrs. Moffatt suddenly remembered the beautiful red wool coat she had bought on sale last spring. She wore it over to Mr. Peterson's. She knocked on his door.

"Good morning, dear Jane!" he said.

"Good morning, dear George!" she said.

"Have you decided?" he asked.

"Yes," she said. "I have."

"Well, come in," he said, "and tell me about it. I have made raspberry muffins."

Mrs. Moffatt smiled, but then she happened to look down. "Oh, dear!" she cried. "I am most distressed! I have lost one of the brass buttons from my coat!"

"It can't be very far," said Mr. Peterson. "Let's retrace your steps." He put one hand over his eyes and gazed out into the bright sunlight down the garden path. "Why, look!" he said. "There it is!" And he hurried down the path in his blue bathrobe and slippers, even though it was very, very cold, and snatched up the shiny brass button, and pressed it into her hand.

"George," said Mrs. Moffatt, as she put the button into her pocket, "my dear friend and neighbor, let me tell you the answer right now. The answer is yes."

While she ate a raspberry muffin, Mr. Peterson sewed the brass button back onto Mrs. Moffatt's coat.

"Thank you," she said.

"I knew it couldn't have gone very far," said Mr. George Peterson.

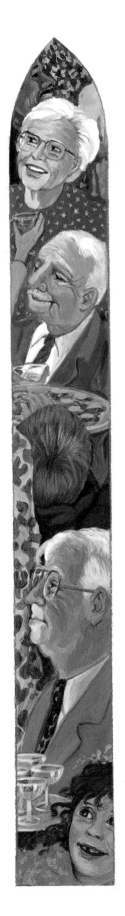

CHAPTER TEN

Holly and Jason Jowarski and their parents, and Mr. and Mrs. Stein and Fred were among the many people from Oak Street and Mrs. Moffatt's school who attended the wedding. Several members of Mr. Peterson's architecture firm, where he had gone back to work, also came. One of them, a Ms. Gloria Turnip, said to Mrs. Moffatt, "I am so glad you have him drawing and designing again. And he seems so happy."

"He is," said Mrs. Moffatt. "And so am I. But you know, sooner or later he would have begun drawing anyway. When you love to do something, sooner or later you do it. It can't go very far."

Ms. Gloria Turnip did not know exactly what Mrs. Moffatt meant, but she said, "Oh yes, certainly."

Also attending the wedding were Mr. Peterson's uncle Phineas, as well as his cousin Hedley, and Mrs. Moffatt's aunt Lucretia. Cousin Hedley gave the couple a chinchilla for their wedding present.

During the Christmas vacation, Jason Jowarski walked up Oak Street every day and fed Puffball the cat and the new chinchilla, whose name was Sidney. This was so Mrs. Jane Moffatt-Peterson and Mr. George Peterson-Moffatt could go on their honeymoon.

They went to Tibet, and when they woke up in their yurt on the first day of the month of the new year, they both remembered to say "Rabbit, rabbit" first thing, for good luck.